D0296515

Felix Takes the Blame

by Maeve Friel

Illustrated by Beccy Blake

W

FRANKLIN WATTS

LONDON • SYDNEY

First published in 2010 by
Franklin Watts
338 Euston Road
London
NW1 3BH

Franklin Watts Australia
Level 17/207 Kent Street
Sydney
NSW 2000

Text © Maeve Friel 2010
Illustration © Beccy Blake 2010

The rights of Maeve Friel to be identified as the author
and Beccy Blake as the illustrator of this Work have been
asserted in accordance with the Copyright, Designs and
Patents Act, 1988.

All rights reserved. No part of this publication may be
reproduced, stored in a retrieval system, or transmitted
in any form or by any means, electronic, mechanical,
photocopy, recording or otherwise, without the prior
written permission of the copyright owner.

A CIP catalogue record for this book is available
from the British Library.

ISBN 978 0 7496 9456 2 (hbk)
ISBN 978 0 7496 9466 1 (pbk)

Series Editor: Jackie Hamley
Series Advisor: Catherine Glavina
Series Designer: Peter Scoulding

Printed in China

Franklin Watts is a divison of
Hachette Children's Books,
an Hachette UK company.
www.hachette.co.uk

ROTHERHAM LIBRARY SERVICE	
B517867	
Bertrams	08/12/2010
JF	£8.99

For Ciara Maeve Kennedy
with love from Granny Maeve

Felix got blamed
for everything.

"FELIX! Where's Felix? Did you do this?" shouted Mum.

"Me? No. No. I didn't do it!"
Felix protested.

Oh no! Not again!

"Look at these sheets!" said
Dad. "Where's that cat?"

"But it wasn't me. I didn't do it!" miaowed Felix.

11

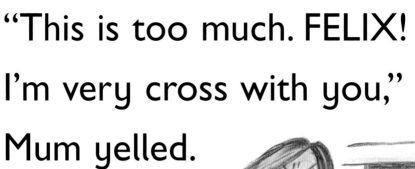

"This is too much. FELIX!
I'm very cross with you,"
Mum yelled.

12

13

"But I wasn't even here!"
Felix fumed.

"Honestly! Felix, I've told you before. You must not dig up my tomato plants," grumbled Dad.

"But it wasn't me! I never dig up the plants! It was Buster!"

Felix was very angry.

"Why do I always get the blame?" he miaowed crossly.

"What a mess!" said Mum. "It can't be – poo. Oh really, Felix. You're disgraceful."

Felix stopped washing his face. "I didn't do it," he miaowed. "It wasn't me. Not me. Never."

25

Suki the kitten was
chasing a butterfly.

Felix pointed a paw.
"It was ..."

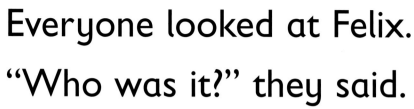

Everyone looked at Felix.
"Who was it?" they said.

Felix looked at Suki.

"It was me," he miaowed.

And he turned a little red.

29

Puzzle 1

Put these pictures in the correct order.
Now tell the story in your own words.
How short can you make the story?

Puzzle 2

upset   confused

delighted

angry   tired

cross

Choose the words which best describe each character. Can you think of any more? Pretend to be one of the characters!

Answers

Puzzle 1

The correct order is:

1c, 2f, 3a, 4e, 5d, 6b

Puzzle 2

Felix The correct words are confused, upset.

The incorrect word is delighted.

Mum The correct words are angry, cross.

The incorrect word is tired.

Look out for more Leapfrog stories:

The Little Star
ISBN 978 0 7496 3833 7

Mary and the Fairy
ISBN 978 0 7496 9142 4

Jack's Party
ISBN 978 0 7496 4389 8

Pippa and Poppa
ISBN 978 0 7496 9140 0

The Bossy Cockerel
ISBN 978 0 7496 9141 7

The Best Snowman
ISBN 978 0 7496 9143 1

Big Bad Blob
ISBN 978 0 7496 7092 4*
ISBN 978 0 7496 7796 1

Cara's Breakfast
ISBN 978 0 7496 7797 8

Croc's Tooth
ISBN 978 0 7496 7799 2

The Magic Word
ISBN 978 0 7496 7800 5

Tim's Tent
ISBN 978 0 7496 7801 2

Why Not?
ISBN 978 0 7496 7798 5

Sticky Vickie
ISBN 978 0 7496 7986 6

Handyman Doug
ISBN 978 0 7496 7987 3

Billy and the Wizard
ISBN 978 0 7496 7985 9

Sam's Spots
ISBN 978 0 7496 7984 2

Bill's Baggy Trousers
ISBN 978 0 7496 3829 0

Bill's Bouncy Shoes
ISBN 978 0 7496 7990 3

Bill's Scary Backpack
ISBN 978 0 7496 9458 6*
ISBN 978 0 7496 9468 5

Little Joe's Big Race
ISBN 978 0 7496 3832 0

Little Joe's Balloon Race
ISBN 978 0 7496 7989 7

Little Joe's Boat Race
ISBN 978 0 7496 9457 9*
ISBN 978 0 7496 9467 8

Felix on the Move
ISBN 978 0 7496 4387 4

Felix and the Kitten
ISBN 978 0 7496 7988 0

Felix Takes the Blame
ISBN 978 0 7496 9456 2*
ISBN 978 0 7496 9466 1

The Cheeky Monkey
ISBN 978 0 7496 3830 6

Cheeky Monkey on Holiday
ISBN 978 0 7496 7991 0

Cheeky Monkey's Treasure Hunt
ISBN 978 0 7496 9455 5*
ISBN 978 0 7496 9465 4

For details of all our titles go to: www.franklinwatts.co.uk

*hardback